To Nick & Jack

Hello from the
Fuji Film Blimp

Captain Mike

Henry's SKY SHIP!

WRITTEN *and* ILLUSTRATED *by* MICHAEL FREIMUTH

An Airship Management Services Publication

Airship Management Services · The Skycruiser Group
2 Soundview Drive · Greenwich, CT 06830

Printed and bound in the United States of America · First Edition
Words in bold type are defined in the glossary or technical pages.

For
the real Henry,
Caroline and Thomas.
And for Nicky,
Isabella and Peter.

It started out like any other warm, sunny summer day. Henry decided to go for a walk in the field behind his house, like he always did.

There's a slight breeze coming off the grassy plains – perfect for playing with his glider. Henry throws his little wooden plane up and over a ridge, where it lands in some tall grass. He likes to pretend it's one of the airplanes from the airfield near his house. As he picks up his plane, Henry looks across the field – and sees something magical!

Vera fotog

"It's a skyship!" he shouts. There in front of him, tethered to a truck with a tall mast, Henry sees a big red blimp swaying slowly in the warm afternoon breeze.

Henry approaches the blimp with growing excitement. He can barely contain himself as he walks around the towering expanse of red. "This is the first time I've seen a skyship at my airport!" Henry thinks. He sees wires, trucks, cones, and a heap of little red bags. He tries to lift one off the ground but can only pull it up a bit. "It's so heavy!" he thinks.

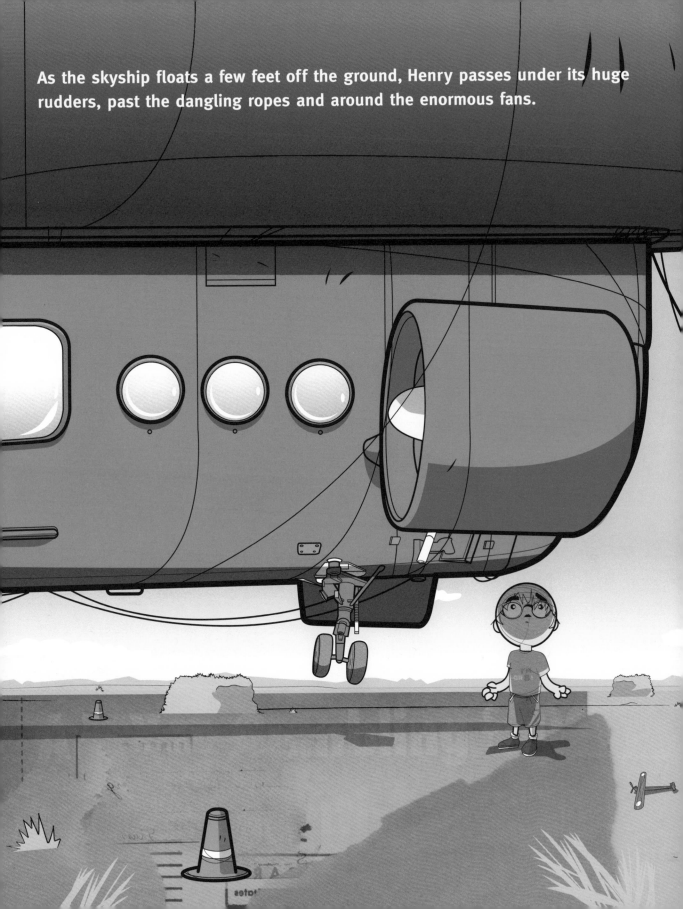

As the skyship floats a few feet off the ground, Henry passes under its huge rudders, past the dangling ropes and around the enormous fans.

Walking around the front of the cabin, he almost trips over a ladder that leads inside. The skyship moves slowly, rotating on its tether, rising ever so gently with the wind.

"I'm aboard! I can't believe I'm actually inside a blimp!" Henry sees rows of big leather seats to the right, the pilots' cockpit to his left.

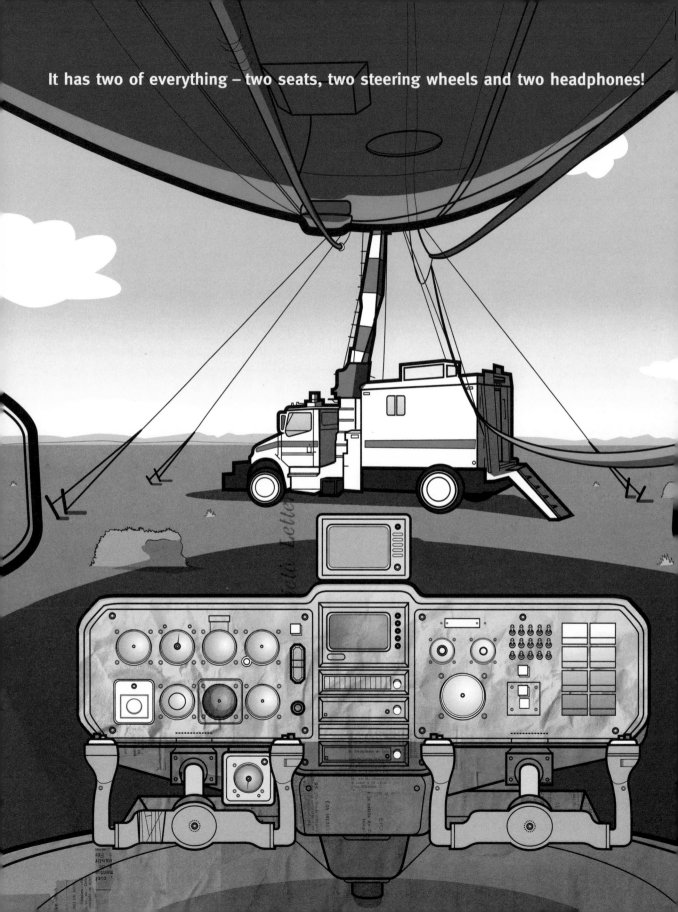

It has two of everything – two seats, two steering wheels and two headphones!

Henry plops down behind a wheel, ready to fly. He puts on the headphones and pulls the levers, snaps the buttons and toggles the switches. "I'm the captain, and I'll fly on out of here!"

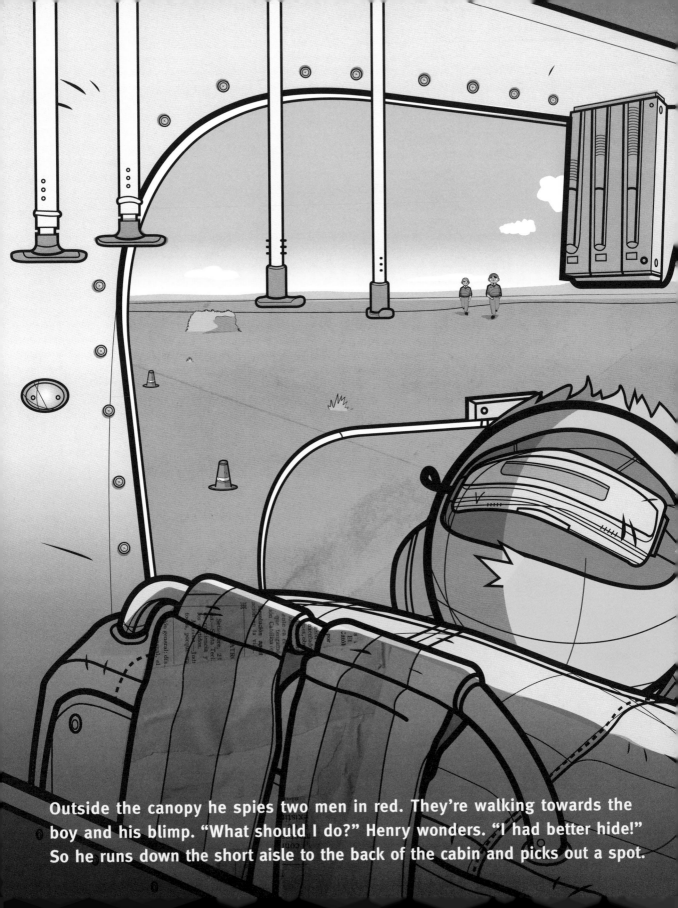

Outside the canopy he spies two men in red. They're walking towards the boy and his blimp. "What should I do?" Henry wonders. "I had better hide!" So he runs down the short aisle to the back of the cabin and picks out a spot.

He finds a blanket and quickly pulls it over himself. "I'm hidden," he thinks, and then he stays perfectly still, silent as a mouse. It's dark under the blanket and he can't see a thing.

Suddenly, voices grow nearer. Steps are climbed ... buttons, toggles and levers are flipped, caught and switched. The blimp starts to hum and Henry hears other noises all around. A few minutes tick by ... "Should I come out of hiding?" he wonders. But just as he is about to, he hears someone yell "Upship!" The seat lurches back and he's too late!

He looks out of the window and sees that they're climbing, flying away! He spots his tiny wooden glider far away, and then it's gone, too small! People and trucks are shrinking – everything is so little! Up, up they go … up, up, up!

The town and countryside are unfolding below, spreading out towards the horizon. "This is amazing!" he thinks.

He hears rumbling, fumbling from the front, static and chirps, beeps and pops. Still under the blanket on the seat, Henry peeks around the corner of the chair – to see a man standing above him. His bright white shirt has a sparkling silver pin with wings on it and a picture of the skyship in the middle.

"We have a stowaway!" the man calls to the front. He looks down at the boy and smiles, "What's your name?" Henry doesn't say a word. "Don't worry, we aren't going to throw you out!" he laughs kindly.

"My name is Henry," says Henry.
"Well Henry, I'm Captain Mike. I don't know how you got on board – I wonder what we're going to do with you? ... I know, how would you like to be our First Mate today?"

Henry looks unsure ... the Captain unhooks his pin and gently clips the wings onto Henry's shirt. "What do you think?" Captain Mike asks.
Now it's Henry's turn to smile. "Okay!" he says.
"Well then," says Mike, "welcome aboard our skyship!"

Henry walks with Mike toward the cockpit. "This part of the blimp we're in now is called the **gondola** and the big inflatable part is called the **envelope**," says Mike. "If you have any questions, just ask!"

Mike motions for Henry to sit down in the co-pilot's chair – next to a friendly looking man.

"Hi there," says the man, "I'm John, and I suppose you're our new First Mate!"
"Yes sir," nods Henry enthusiastically. He can't believe how lucky he is!
"A little while ago, I was playing in the field," he thinks to himself, "and now I'm the First Mate on a skyship!"

Sitting down in the cockpit once again, Henry sees the same buttons, panels, and lights as before. Only this time they're actually working!

"That's the **altimeter**," John says, pointing to the numbers on the spinning dial. "Right now we're 1000 feet up. The rest of these instruments help us navigate and monitor the blimp, so that we can fly safely."

Henry looks around, overwhelmed. "How could you ever keep so many buttons straight?"

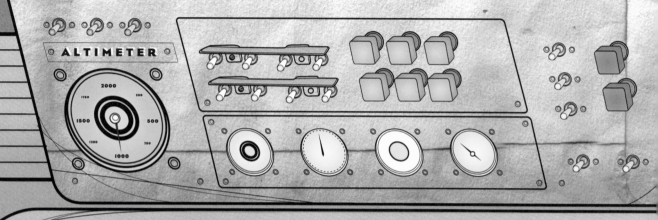

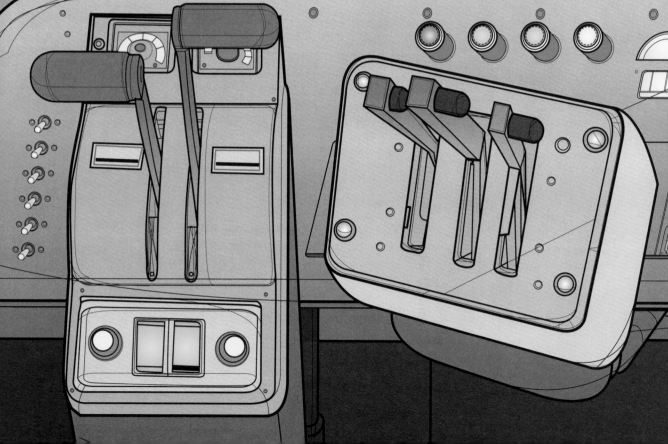

"You know, Henry," says Mike, "the best way to learn about the blimp is to fly it. How would you like to give it a whirl?"

Henry's already big smile grows bigger as he shouts, "Would I!?"

"Well then, just grab the **yoke**!" John laughs, pointing to the steering wheel.

Henry slowly takes the handles, they're big in his hands, but not hard to turn. He remembers when his Dad let him steer the motor boat on the lake last summer – and that's exactly what it feels like – as if he's driving a boat, a really big boat!

Mike points to the right, **starboard** as he calls it (just like on the water), and nods. Henry turns the yoke to the right. It's slow at first, and then the great skyship banks, curving out over a small lake with little sailboats on it.

The water looks like glass from this high up. Henry sees the tiny dinghies with their tiny passengers – he waves excitedly to the people down below!

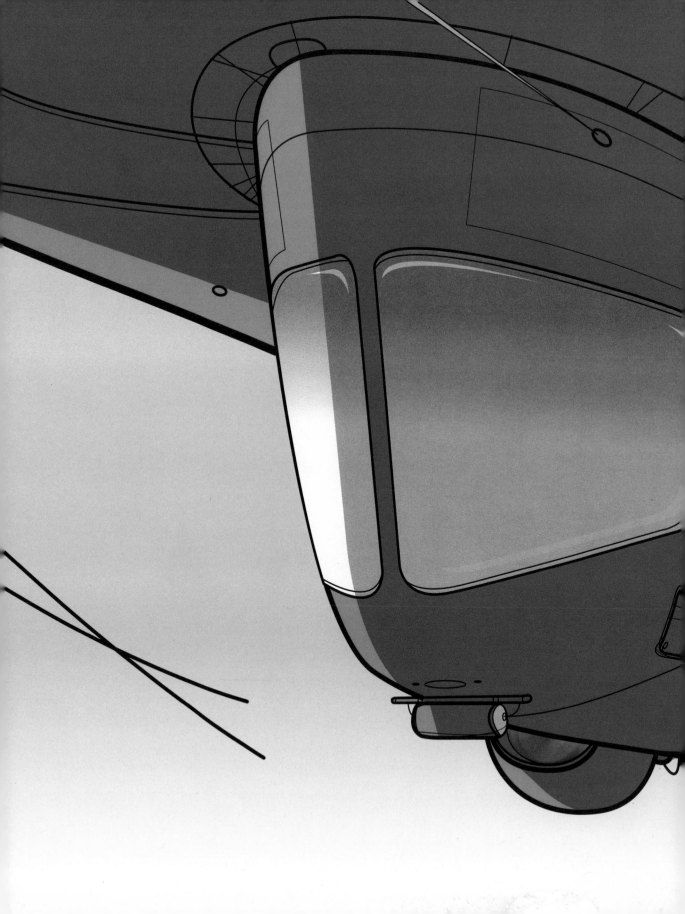

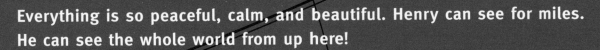

Everything is so peaceful, calm, and beautiful. Henry can see for miles.
He can see the whole world from up here!

John and Mike ask Henry if he has any questions. "Well, how do you like it?"
they ask. "Do you want to know how it works?"
"Of course!" Henry says. He wants to know all about his skyship, he can't
wait to tell his brother and sister about this adventure.

"Well," Mike says, "we share the skies with a lot of other aircraft." He tells Henry how the blimp stays at airfields and airports across the country. "Usually they're smaller airfields so that the blimp doesn't get in the way of the big jets. We often share the field with biplanes and private gliders." "And you go all over the country?" asks Henry.

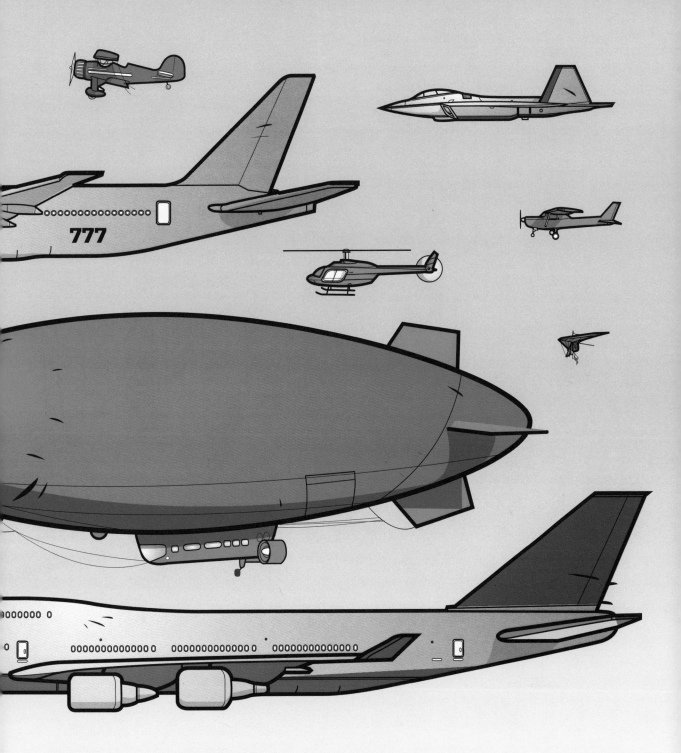

"Yes, we travel with the warm weather, kind of like birds, like a giant bird really. We migrate!" he laughs. "We like to stay with the good weather. It's difficult to fly in the snow or rain; we like the wind on our side!" Henry smiles with the Captains; he loves it up here – he loves flying like a bird.

John reaches up to some metal tubes with handles on the end and pulls one. "What are those for? Are they for the big engines?" Henry asks hopefully. "No Henry," John says, smiling. "These are for the **ballonets**." He points to a white cable outside the cockpit's bubble that leads to a metal circle. "If I pull this," he pulls a lever down, "the wire pops open that valve and lets out air." Henry watches as John pulls down and a metal circle flops down in front of them, underneath the blimp.

"There's one in the back too. We let out the air to equalize the pressure because the **helium** expands as we go higher. You see, there are two big compartments in the envelope – balloons inside balloons. These help

Ballonets

Skyships are equipped with a pair of ballonets, one forward, one aft. These air-filled compartments are used primarily to control and regulate envelope pressure. Ballonets can also act as ballast tanks and can be differentially inflated to control **trim**.

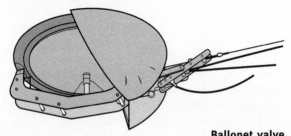

Ballonet valve

Ascending (Helium expands)

The ballonet valves release air, (denoted by shaded area).

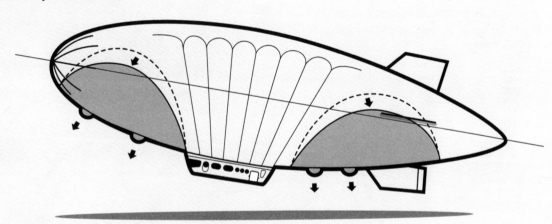

Descending (Helium contracts)

The air is driven back into the ballonets through the **air ducts** by motorized pumps.

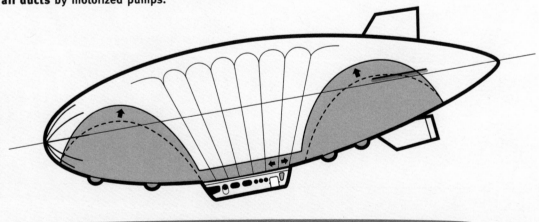

Engines

The skyship has two 6-cylinder, air-cooled, turbo-charged engines producing around 255 horse-power. This allows the blimp a cruising speed of 35 to 40 miles per hour, and a maximum velocity of 65 miles per hour, depending on the wind.

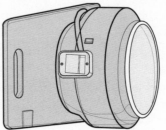

Air duct

Vectors

The skyship has two variable pitch propellers that allow it to fly straight, hover, or move anywhere in between. This is known as **vectored thrust**, which allows for a smooth and surprisingly rapid take-off and landing.

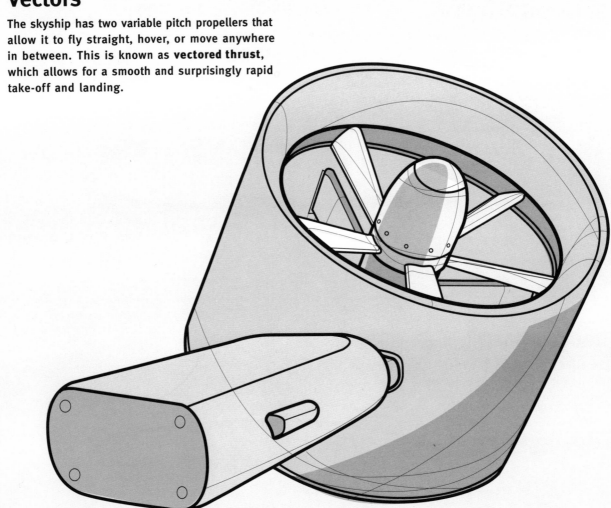

"Those engines we've got are turbos – like the ones from race cars," says Mike. "The **vectors** can rotate so we can fly straight or hover, like we do at football and baseball games. Sometimes we carry a big camera that lets us zoom in and see the action the way nobody else does." Henry likes baseball, and that sounds like fun!

"Today we'll only be up for an hour," says John. "And lucky for you too! We don't want your parents getting worried with you being gone."
"It's okay," says Henry. His brother and sister were having a picnic with his parents back home. He regularly went on walks, throwing his wooden glider as he went along. No one minded if he was gone for a little while. "What a surprise they'll have when I get back and tell them about this!" he thinks.

"Today we're just flying so that people can see us," says John, "which is called **exposure**. But sometimes we have a lot more fun than that! We do all sorts of things!"

And with that, John tells Henry about the places they've been and the things they've seen. All their trips across the country, through the desert, over the mountains and seas, and above the dozens of cities they see every year during the thousands of miles they fly. It sounded like John and Mike had been just about everywhere. Henry tries to imagine all their adventures.

"What's your favorite place?" Henry asks.

"Well there's always something new to see, but I especially love Cape Cod," says John.

He tells Henry about the whale watching they do along the coast, how they help the scientists monitor the whales as they migrate. "We were so low over those big whales that we could hear them singing to each other!"

"Sometimes we work with the police to patrol cities and waterways, and once we caught a runaway boat!" exclaims John excitedly. He tells Henry how he flew down low over a fleeing motorboat and shone a spotlight on the driver just as it went underneath them. "It must have scared him half to death," laughs John. "And gave the police boats enough time to catch up with him."

"A blimp can do a lot of things that other aircraft can't, like hover and be silent. Why, we could hover in one spot all day long and you would barely hear us – we could be right above you!"

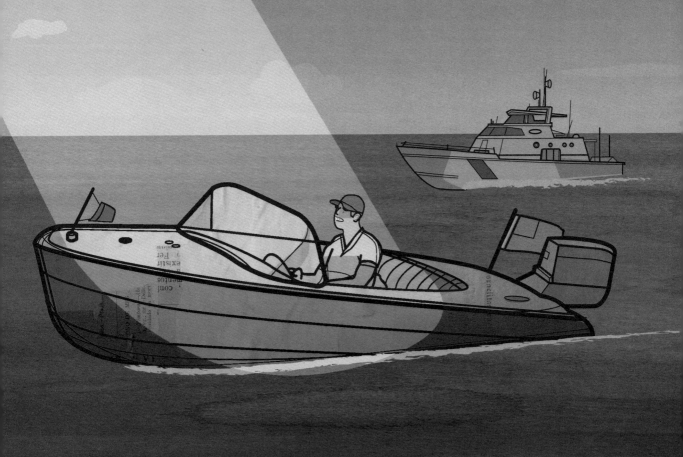

"Every year we travel back to our huge hangar in Elizabeth City, North Carolina. You could fit lots of skyships in there if you packed them in." Henry tries to imagine the hangar with all its blimps – it seems that it must be bigger than anything he's ever seen.

John tells him of the old friends they see every year and the new people they meet as their journeys unfold: how one time the skyship landed in a field full of cows. It was a small town, and all the folks came over to see the amazing blimp as it stood peacefully in the pasture.

Mike gazes out to **port** at the low clouds off in the distance. "I love the blimp. No one in the world gets to see the things the way we do. We're lucky," he says, smiling at Henry and John, "to be part of something so magical."

Henry feels the same way. The warm sunshine falls on his face as he gazes out of the open window to where Mike is looking. He sees the earth stretch out forever, the towns, fields and trees fading into the distance as far as he can see. Everything seems so wonderful up here.

John glances over at Mike. "Shall we turn this thing around?" he asks Henry. Henry nods, "Okay."

As the great skyship slowly continues on in the afternoon sky, John and Mike explain how the ground crew works so hard to keep everything going, all the people and effort it takes to make this wonderful ship fly every day. They answer more questions about the equipment, trucks, and all the other things on the blimp that Henry wants to know about...

Mobile Mast

A member of the ground crew climbs the mobile mast to detach it from the blimp after the signal to de-mast is given. Whenever the blimp is on the ground for any length of time, it is firmly attached to the mast to keep it from going anywhere. The mast itself is then attached to and controlled by a large truck, which is secured to the ground with strong steel wires and **tensioners**.

Equipment Truck

The ground crew travels in a caravan of vans, cars, and trucks as they follow the skyship across the country. This truck stores some of the many supplies needed for skyship operation.

Skyship Equipment

A skyship's crew travels with all the equipment they might need as they move across the country. This includes anything from everyday tools and machines, to specially designed electronics for blimp maintenance.

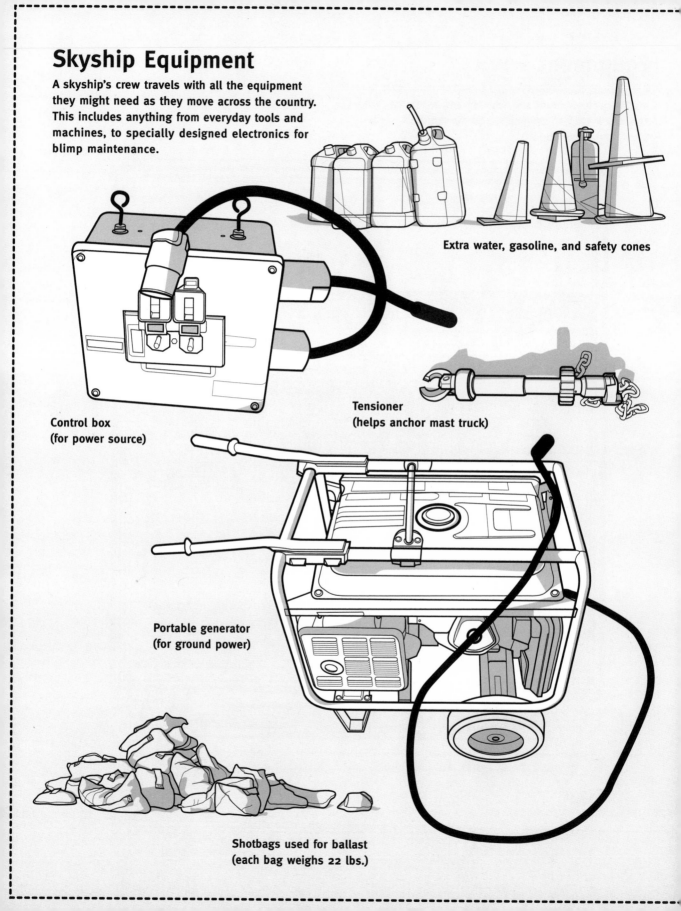

Extra water, gasoline, and safety cones

Control box
(for power source)

Tensioner
(helps anchor mast truck)

Portable generator
(for ground power)

Shotbags used for ballast
(each bag weighs 22 lbs.)

The Crew

It takes an incredible amount of work to keep the skyship up and running all year round. It's all made possible thanks to the pilots and ground crew.

"Thank you for teaching me so much about the skyship," says Henry, "I can't wait to tell my family everything!" The Captains both smile, and Mike points out of the window. As Henry looks down below, he sees the airfield approaching and the tiny radar dish rotating on top of the tower – "We're almost back!" he shouts.

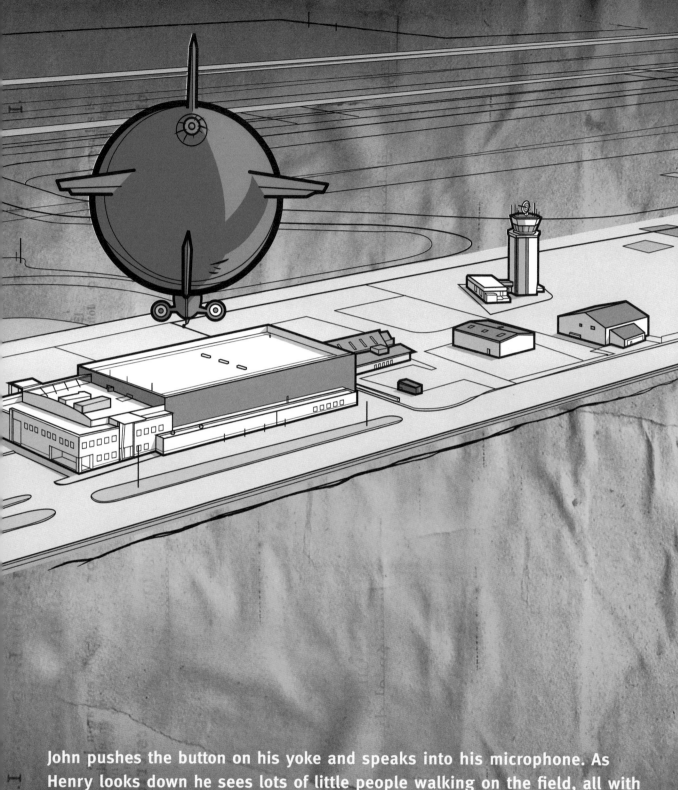

John pushes the button on his yoke and speaks into his microphone. As Henry looks down he sees lots of little people walking on the field, all with their tiny red shirts. "That's the blimp crew!" says John. The crew looks up as the skyship goes over them. Henry looks down and waves, and they all wave back!

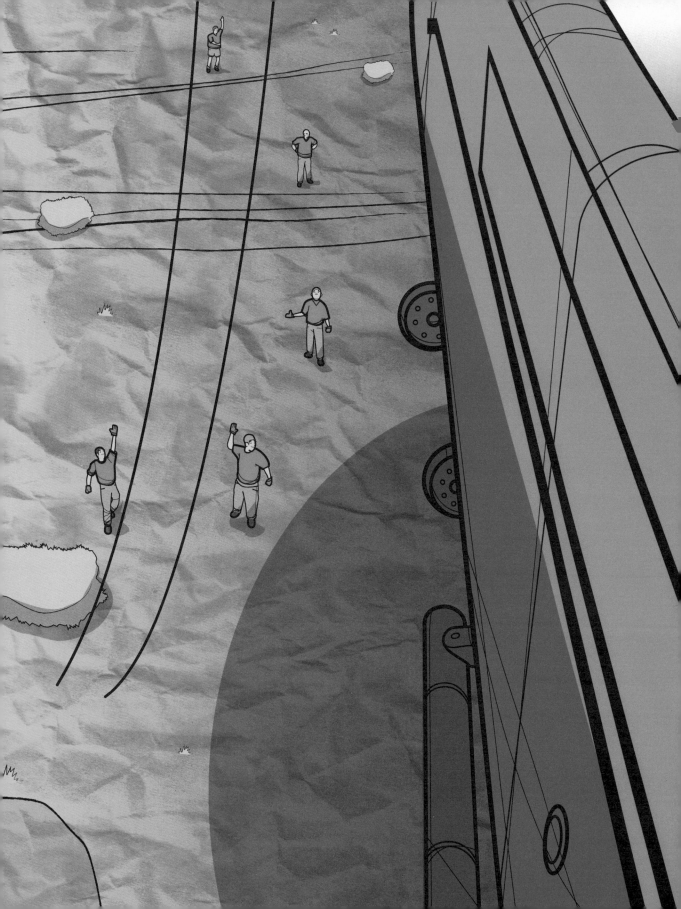

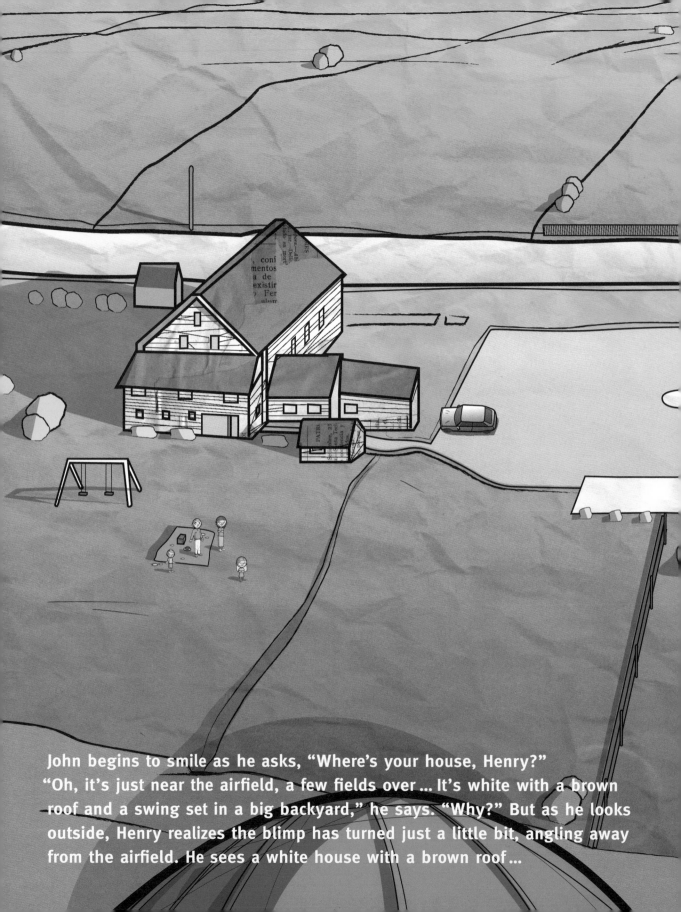

John begins to smile as he asks, "Where's your house, Henry?"
"Oh, it's just near the airfield, a few fields over ... It's white with a brown roof and a swing set in a big backyard," he says. "Why?" But as he looks outside, Henry realizes the blimp has turned just a little bit, angling away from the airfield. He sees a white house with a brown roof ...

And then he sees his family! They look up from their picnic of bread, jams and lemonade as the blimp slowly comes to a stop above them. Henry pokes his head out the window and sees the shocked look on everyone's faces! He smiles back at John and Mike, who laugh. His brother and sister keep pointing, and when they see Henry, they jump up, waving and shouting.

Slowly the blimp lowers itself to the ground, the **landing gear** flexing softly on its spring. Its enormous shape fits easily into their big backyard. As the skyship touches down, Henry sees the amazement on everyone's face.

Henry looks over at the Captains and they nod to him. He gets up, puts his headphones away, and moves toward the door as Mike opens it for him. Henry remembers the pin on his shirt and reaches to take it off, but Mike stops him. "Keep it," he says with a smile, "to remember our voyage." Henry salutes John and Mike – who salute him back with smiles on their faces.

He jumps off the stairs and runs over to his parents. With that, the great skyship's engines power up and it lifts off the ground. It pulls up – up over the yard and the trees, up high above the roof and then turns slowly back toward the airfield in a widening circle.

Henry waves goodbye as his brother and sister race over to him, shouting questions. Henry just smiles as he watches the skyship climb into the sky and disappear past the trees.

**THE
END**

Glossary Airship to Zeppelin

Airship: A balloon or envelope filled with a lighter-than-air gas, which gives it lift. It is powered by motors and steered by control surfaces or fins; it usually houses a gondola or cabin underneath. Airship is another name for skyship.

Altimeter: An instrument used by the pilot to determine the height of the airship above sea level. It senses changes in atmospheric pressure as the airship ascends and descends and registers these as changes in altitude.

Ballast: Everything on or inside the airship, including the helium and the air in the ballonets. "Disposable ballast" takes the form of water or shotbags. Dropping disposable ballast enables an airship to ascend or to compensate for helium loss or an increased payload.

Blimp: An airship that has no internal framework to maintain the shape of the envelope. Blimps are also called non-rigid, or pressure airships.

Buoyancy: The force that allows an airship to float in the air. This force comes from the air surrounding the airship in exactly the same way as buoyancy comes from the water surrounding a boat or submarine. The amount of buoyant force depends upon how much outside air the airship pushes aside or displaces. The bigger the airship, the greater the buoyant force.

Cables: Long steel ropes used to activate valves or control surfaces from the cockpit.

Center of Buoyancy: The center of the volume of the air that is displaced by the airship's envelope. Since the shape of the envelope cannot be changed, the location of the center of buoyancy cannot be changed.

Center of Gravity (CG): The point inside the airship where its entire weight is said to be concentrated. On Henry's skyship, the center of gravity is located a short distance above the gondola and in between the forward and rear ballonets. The entire airship is just like a see-saw hinged at this point.

Dirigible: Another word for "airship." It comes from the French "dirigeable," which means steerable or capable of being directed or guided.

Dynamic Lift: The aerodynamic lift generated by flying an airship with its nose up to compensate for heaviness or with its nose down to compensate for lightness.

Elevators: The moveable surfaces attached to an airship's horizontal tail fins used to control nose up and nose down movement.

Envelope: The gasbag, or hull, of a non-rigid airship.

Equilibrium: When the weight of the airship and its contents equals the weight of the outside air displaced by the envelope. In this condition, the airship's weight is zero.

Exposure: Flights over cities and towns so that large numbers of people can see the airship.

Fins: The fixed vertical and horizontal stabilizing surfaces attached to an airship's tail.

Gondola: The part of the airship that carries the pilots, passengers, payload, cabin and engines. It is always located on the bottom of the airship.

Gross Lift: The gross lift is equal to the total buoyant force acting on the airship minus the weight of the gasses inside the airship.

Helium: An odorless and non-flammable gas; it is the second lightest element known. Helium is used to inflate the fabric envelope, creating a light but strong structure.

Kevlar: A composite material used in the production of both the cables and gondola of an airship.

Landing Gear: The wheel-based mechanism below the gondola upon which the airship pivots and lands.

Manometer: An instrument used by the pilot to monitor the pressures of the helium and ballonet air.

Non-rigid Airship: An airship or blimp with no internal structure and an envelope made of light-weight, gas-tight fabric.

Port: When standing in the gondola, facing toward the front of the airship, the port side of the airship is to the left.

Pressure Height: The maximum height that an airship can ascend to before decreasing atmospheric pressure causes the ballonets to become completely empty.

Rigid Airship: An airship constructed from a rigid framework of metal or wood and covered with fabric. The helium is contained inside a number of drum shaped gasbags attached to the inside of the frame.

Rudders: The moveable surfaces attached to an airship's vertical tail fins used for steering left or right.

Semi-Rigid Airship: An airship similar to a non-rigid except with a "keel" along the bottom of the envelope to help spread the load of the gondola more evenly.

Starboard: When standing in the gondola, facing toward the front of the airship, the starboard side of the airship is to the right.

Trim: When the vessel is in level flight, with no deflection of the elevators, it is "in trim." When inclined down by either the bow or stern, it is "out of trim." An airship's trim is adjusted by moving air between the two ballonets.

Viewing Dome: A large, dome shaped window located in the ceiling of the gondola. The pilots and crew look through this window to see how much air is contained inside the ballonets.

Vectored Thrust: The directional thrust from swiveling propeller ducts, permitting an airship to take-off and land at various static weights without long take-off and landing runs.

Weigh Off: The process of assessing an airship's static weight and trim condition. Weigh Offs are normally performed on the ground, just before take-off, and in flight, just before landing.

Yoke: The steering wheel of the airship. It controls the rudders and elevators.

Zeppelin: Any rigid airship manufactured by the company founded by Count Ferdinand von Zeppelin in Friedrichshafen, Germany in 1908. The world famous Graf Zeppelin, and ill-fated Hindenburg were both Zeppelin airships. Because they are rigid airships, Zeppelins are technically not "blimps."

Thank You

Many thanks are owed to all who helped make this book a reality. Thanks to George Spyrou for this wonderful opportunity. Thank you also to Adam Berninger, Josh Lebowitz, and Natalie Thomas my unofficial editors; to my family, Stanley, Sarah, Alex, and Rudy; to Mike Fitzpatrick, John McGuirk, John McHugh, Scott Danneker, Bill Armstrong, and the entire Airship Fuji ground crew of Airship Management Services; to Fuji Photo Film U.S.A, for helping me to tell this story. Lastly, thank you to Henry himself, for the inspiration, and who hopefully will not grow out of this story too quickly.